this
·little·barron's·
book belongs to

Marissa

Pernatin

First edition for the United States and Canada published 1999
by Barron's Educational Series, Inc.

Text copyright © Sally Grindley 1997
Illustrations copyright © Andy Ellis 1997

First published in Great Britain by Orchard Books in 1997

All inquiries should be addressed to:
Barron's Educational Series, Inc.
250 Wireless Boulevard
Hauppauge, New York 11788
http://www.barronseduc.com

Library of Congress Catalog Card No.: 98-72770
International Standard Book No. 0-7641-0860-3

Printed in Italy

987654321

Elephant Small
Is Lost

by **Sally Grindley**

illustrated by **Andy Ellis**

• little • barron's •

Elephant Small was lost.
  "Where are you, Elephant
Small?" sobbed Elephant Mom.
  But there was no reply.

Jolly Dog came bounding to the rescue. "Don't worry, Elephant Mom, I'll soon sniff him out!" he said.

And he bounced off around the room.

Jolly Dog sniffed through
Dumpy Truck's bricks.
SNIFF SNIFF – OUCH!

BONK!

But Elephant Small wasn't there.

Jolly Dog sniffed behind Jack-in-the-Box.
SNIFF SNIFF – OOOH!

BOING!

But Elephant Small wasn't there.

Jolly Dog sniffed through Big Red
Tractor's straw.
SNIFF SNIFF – AATCHOO!

But Elephant Small wasn't there.

"Where can he be?" sobbed Elephant Mom.

"Where can he be?" said the other toys.

Then they heard a little voice.

"I want my mommy!" it said.

Jolly Dog gave one enormous sniff ...
SNIFF!

and bounced over to the chest of drawers.

SNIFF!

It was Elephant Small.
   "There you are!" cried Elephant Mom
   "Mommy!" cried Elephant Small.
"I got stuck!"

"Thank you, Jolly Dog," said
Elephant Mom. "You are clever!"

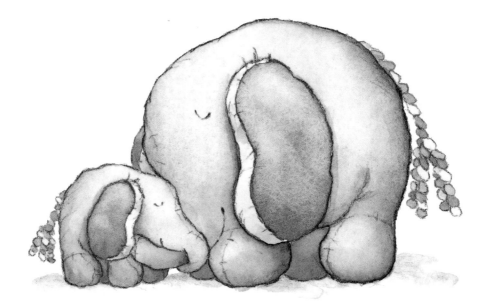